Who Owns

written by Sonia Leviti

PARNASSUS PRES

the Moon?

Illustrated by John Larrecq

BERKELEY, CALIFORNIA

To Danny and Shari

In a far away village carved into a mountainside lived three farmers, Abel, Nagel and Zeke. All day they tilled their fields, and all evening they sat together and argued.

They argued about whose cow gave the richest milk. They argued about whose goat had the strong-

est horns. They argued about whose wife had the loudest voice, the longest nose and the most unpleasant disposition.

"Mine!" cried Abel.

"Mine!" shouted Nagel.

"Mine!" roared Zeke.

They argued until they were tired and went home to bed.

One night when they had argued about every-
thing, and there seemed to be nothing left, Abel
looked up at the moon.

It was a round, full, golden moon, bright and
delicious.

Abel gazed at the moon and sighed, "Mine."

"It's mine!" shouted Nagel.

"No, mine," roared Zeke. "I saw it first."

That night they argued nearly until dawn, and the next night and the next.

By and by the moon waned, until it was only half as large as before.

"My moon," cried Abel. "My moon is melting!"

"That's my moon," shouted Nagel, "and some-one has nibbled half of it away!"

"It's my moon," roared Zeke. "Someone has stolen a big chunk. Help! Thief!"

By and by the moon waned, until only a quarter was left.

"My moon is vanishing," sobbed Abel. "It's

nearly all melted away."

"My moon," shouted Nagel. "Someone is eating it all up."

"It's my moon," roared Zeke. "That thief has stolen most of it, and I will catch him."

By and by the moon shone whole again, but the
argument did not stop.

"Ah, my moon has returned," sighed Abel.

"My moon!" shouted Nagel.

"*My* moon!" roared Zeke.

Never had they argued so loud and so long over
one thing. They did not tend their fields. They did

not mend their fences. Their animals ran wild.
At last their wives decided on a plan. They would

send their husbands down the mountain to the Teacher. Let the Teacher settle the argument once and for all.

That night each wife spoke to her husband.

"Abel, dear husband, you must stop this fighting. You have no time to tend the fields, and we won't have food for next winter. Go down the mountain and talk to the Teacher. He will tell you who owns the moon."

"Nagel, dear husband, this thing must be settled at once. You don't mend your fences. The animals are running wild. Go down the mountain and talk to the Teacher. He will know who really owns the moon."

"Zeke, dear husband, this argument cannot go on. It's making you weary and sick. I hardly see you at home anymore. Go down the mountain and talk to the Teacher. Let him decide who owns the moon."

The three men agreed. The very next day they
went down the mountain to the home of the Teacher. They waited in a long line for a long time.

At last it was their turn. Abel, Nagel and Zeke took off their caps and went inside to tell their problem to the Teacher.

When they had finished, the Teacher sighed. He stroked his beard. He closed his eyes, thinking long and hard. At last he spoke in a deep, resounding voice.

"Abel, Nagel and Zeke," he said, "I know the

answer to this puzzle. The moon belongs to you,
Abel. It belongs to you, Nagel. And it also belongs
to Zeke. The problem is that none of you knows
exactly *when* the moon is his."

Abel, Nagel and Zeke nodded and waited for the
Teacher to continue.

"On Monday and Tuesday," the Teacher told Abel, "the moon belongs to you."

The Teacher said to Nagel, "On Wednesday and Thursday the moon belongs to you."

He told Zeke, "On Friday and Saturday the moon belongs to you."

The Teacher continued. "That leaves only Sunday. On Sunday the moon belongs to everyone."

Abel, Nagel and Zeke bowed down in amazement. Surely the Teacher was the wisest of all wise men.

"One thing more," spoke the Teacher. "The moon will change from full to half to quarter. And on some nights you will not see the moon at all. It will be hiding somewhere in the sky. But it will still be yours. You must do exactly as I tell you. Then the moon will always return full and round."

To Abel he said, "On Monday and Tuesday evenings you must stay home and watch your moon from your own window."

He told Nagel, "On Wednesday and Thursday evenings you must stay home and watch your moon from your own window."

He told Zeke, "On Friday and Saturday evenings you must stay home and watch your moon from your window."

Abel, Nagel and Zeke agreed. "But what," they asked, "shall we do on Sunday?"

"On Sunday evenings," said the Teacher, "you may sit together in peace and be thankful that the

moon is there for everyone."

Abel, Nagel and Zeke bowed low before the Teacher. All the way home up to their village on the mountainside they praised the Teacher and his wisdom.

From then on, every Monday and Tuesday evening, Abel stayed home and sat by his window sighing over the beauty of his moon.

On Wednesday and Thursday evenings Nagel stayed home and sat by his window admiring his marvelous moon.

On Friday and Saturday evenings Zeke stayed home and sat by his window praising his wonderful moon.

On the few nights when they could not see the moon, Abel, Nagel or Zeke would laugh and say, "Ah, my playful moon is hiding in the sky."

Their wives were most contented. No longer did Abel, Nagel and Zeke spend their nights arguing. Instead, they went to bed in time to wake up refreshed the next day, and they tended their fields and mended their fences just as good farmers should.

On the two nights that the moon was his, each farmer was happy. On the other nights he was satisfied, knowing that his turn would come again soon.

But Abel, Nagel and Zeke agreed that the best
night of all was Sunday. For on Sunday they sat
together singing beneath the moon. And it seemed

to them that while the moon was always beautiful,
it was *most* beautiful on the one night when it be-
longed to everyone.

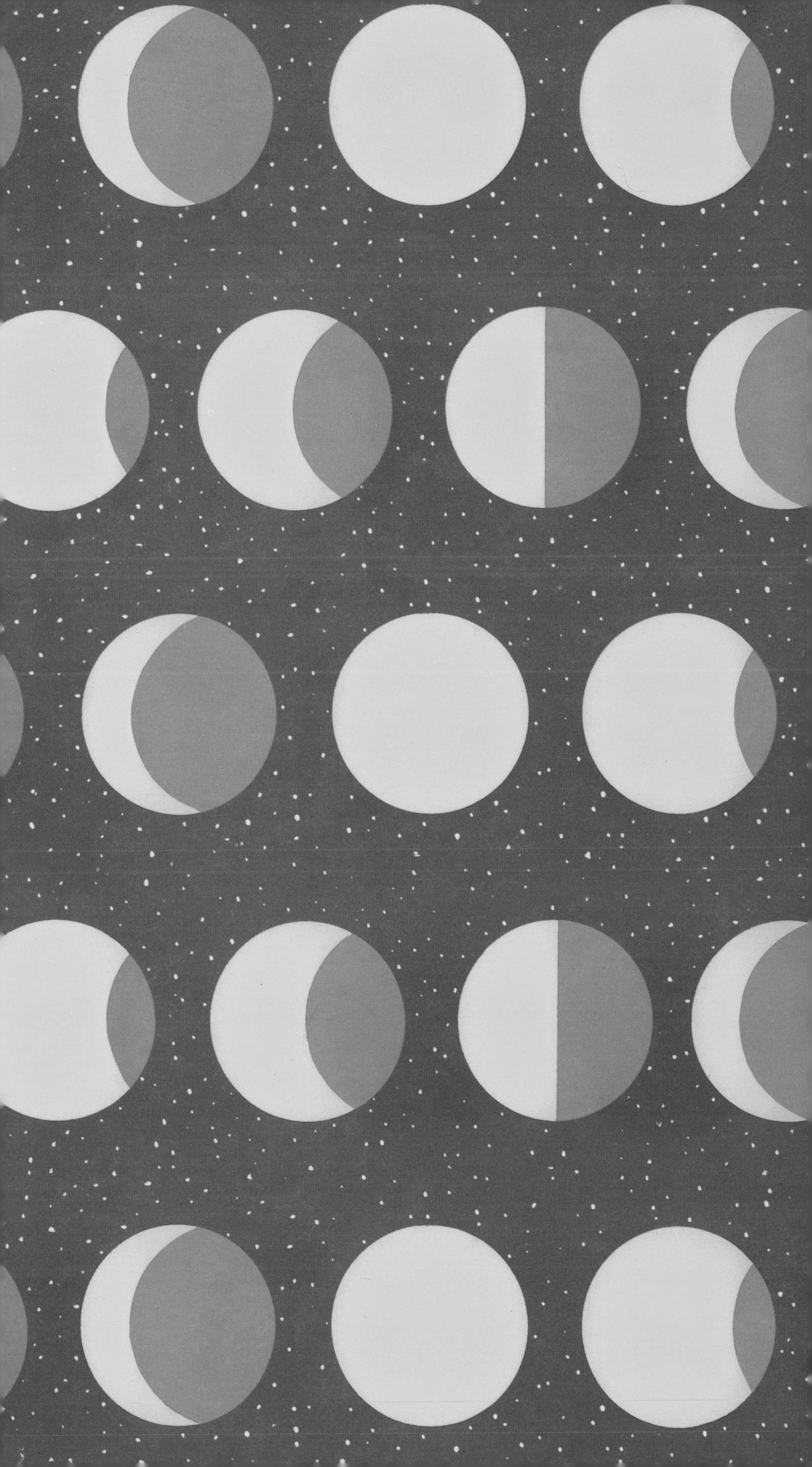